Ukko

By

C Faherty Brown

"Ukko, in Finnish folk religion, the god of thunder, one of the most important deities. The name Ukko is derived from ukkonen, "thunder", but it also means "old man" and is used as a term of respect."

-The Internet

Ukko, he just makes everything better.

-Aada

I.

When I left, I left angry. Disappointed. Frustrated. All of the negative weight one could find, I found, and I carried it. Including blame. I blamed everyone. Myself as well. But in truth, mostly not myself.

It took six months of living alone and depending on no one but myself to come to some realizations. The first thing I got rid of was the blame. Before I moved I had tried therapy. That didn't work, it was too drawn out and too dependent on the therapist's interpretation of what I was saying or not saying. Here, I just flat out faced what was what. I was blaming life in general for how I felt about life in general. I was surprised when I had that realization at how much better I felt.

The best thing to help was chopping wood. Not to knock therapy, it has its place. But when I knew I had to chop wood to stay warm, and I had to make sure I was chopping the right kind of wood so I didn't clog the chimney, and I had to make sure it was seasoned, and I had to do it all alone, I thought a lot. About so much more than any self-wallow-thinking had been about. I couldn't get away from the new thinking. It was a distraction. Not to mention the physical demands. When I started chopping wood, the first time in my life, everything about me hurt. My body hurt. My head hurt. My soul hurt. Until it didn't. My body became conditioned to hauling, cutting, moving the wood. My mind became unconditioned to what I was suppose to think and feel and started thinking freely, started thinking clearly and without the long carried self-imposed burdens.

Once blame dissipated, anger decided to leave with it. I'm pretty sure that half of the anger I carried I didn't even know what it was about. Possibly it was labeled wrong. But it felt like anger. The wood chopping was probably a good part of that release as well. Fortunately I had plenty of land with fallen trees and branches and bramble to clear out. When I moved here and started the very long process of cleaning and clearing and preparing for living alone the 'fuck's and 'mother-fuck's were fast and furious. It was an incredulous realization one day when it occurred to me I hadn't cussed in many days. Things that went wrong and things that just didn't go right weren't eliciting verbal explosions because they were no longer creating inner turmoil.

Physical labor and having to focus on resolutions to basic needs were serving me well.

Frustration just kind of disappeared.

Disappointment sometimes reared up but I was getting better at redirecting it. The most difficult thing about disappointment was realizing how responsible I was for feeling like this, and for so long.

Now, as I stand here, I feel lighter. Mentally because of the weight I have let go of by realizing and taking the responsibility I should have been aware of all along. Physically because the work demands of being here have helped me shed a few pounds.

I hung the splitting maul next to the too-light axe I had initially used to split wood and felt gratification at what I had accomplished. And not too soon with the chill air and near bitter winds that have been whipping through the mountains some days and nights. A couple of days had seen snow flakes but nothing accumulated yet. The propane tank behind the house was full. I hoped to not have to use the propane heat much due to the high cost of filling the tank. But in an emergency or when I had to leave the house without the fire burning it was nice to have a back-up heat source.

I'd done everything I could to be ready for winter on this mountain. My first winter here. My first winter alone. I spent the summer doing as much as I could to the mountain house to winterize it and update what I could, on my own.

I hadn't planned on a divorce. I hadn't planned on living in this mountain house my grandfather left my father, who left it to me years ago. Though I'd been here often growing up and while my grandparents and parents were alive I'd only been here a handful of times since I was a teenager and only a couple of times since my parents died. And then only to check on it. No one lived in it full-time since Granddad's death. My parents used it frequently on weekends and holidays. At times I had considered selling it after they died. More than once, more than one hundred times, I thanked myself for not selling it. I hadn't planned on changing jobs and locations and living a lifestyle unfamiliar to any way I had yet lived. It was one thing to visit and holiday here when someone else was caretaking and doing all of the work. It was altogether something else to live here.

The wood shed was full. The front and back porch had lean-tos built on that were full with wood as well. The bench in the house to store wood for the wood-burning stove was full. The cabinets and make-shift pantry (closet turned pantry) were full of food. The freezer was full. I had a generator in addition to being connected to the grid. I don't mind roughing some things but I want electric and water. Granddad's century-plus old outhouse was still standing and functional with a new toilet seat and fresh paint. But I thanked him again, out loud, for having a bathroom built inside when he no longer wanted Grandma sluffing through snow, ice and muck to go to the bathroom. The outhouse was nice to have when I was outside working and dirty and didn't want to track through the house. The utility room in the house had been fitted with a washer and dryer by dad decades ago. Washer and dryer updated by me.

Spinning slowly I took in the area around the house now clean of nature's debris. Granddad would be proud of the spruce-up I'd given the place. The house showed itself off in a new coat of honey colored stain. I had sealed all of the windows and covered all of the oldest ones with heavy plastic to stop any drafts. Windows will have to be replaced as I saved for them. I refused to go into debt and though I had some money left from the divorce, it wasn't enough to live high on. I considered it my emergency fund. I knew I could live off of my income and even save some if I was careful and mindful of my spending.

So far I had done everything on my own. Every paint brush stroke. Every single stick or log moved and chopped. Every shovel load of gravel tossed into the potholes of the lane that led from the main road.

I was tired. Good and achey tired from the work and the energy expended. I smiled as I walked up on the porch and went inside. My smiles were returning and I felt more...me. The living area and kitchen were one large room. The floors were solid oak planks. The walls were more like panels but also wood. Granddad's Granddad knew what he was doing when he built this tiny castle.   The kitchen was along the back wall of the large room. Cabinets and counter and sink had all been updated by Granddad.   Still 'new' to the house they were now old.   Beautifully built to last.   The south side of the house was two small bedrooms with a bathroom between them.   I suspect the bathroom was built by taking space from each of the bedrooms.   It was spacious enough.   Had an old claw foot tub, toilet, pedestal sink and closet. More than enough for me.

I used the second bedroom as my home office.   Work life changed drastically due to the pandemic. Before I even moved here I was working remote, from home.   Now, I go to the office one, two or three days a week, working from home on the other days. From what the folks on the mountain told me I would be working more from home during the winter because I wouldn't want to drive off the mountain on many days.

I used to live 'on the other side' of the city where I now work. Now I live on 'this side of' the city, on a mountain, with more distance between me and work. And come the snow, my commute will take even longer. I didn't mind the distance. Especially because I didn't have to do it every day. And usually it was my choice to go to work or work from home. The benefits of the tech world are sometimes overlooked or unseen compared to the negative worlds that have been created online. I don't participate in any of it any longer. After the divorce, or during it, I disconnected from any and all social media. Talk about getting rid of frustration and despair. Youtube was my friend for researching how to do things and find out how others are living in remote or isolated areas. I wasn't necessarily isolated unless I compared it to how I lived in a city with neighbors just feet away. Now my closest neighbor was almost a mile away in one direction. Half a mile in another direction. But I knew everyone in an almost five mile radius. At the very least I knew their names. Before, in an area where people were 'more' I didn't know but one neighbor in any radius configuration.

My home was sparsely furnished compared to my previous homes. It suited me. Or I suited it. The importance of stuff lost its allure to me when during the divorce 'things' were argued over more than the loss of our relationship. I struggled to understand how he was so attached to our belongings but not enough to our relationship to argue over it. Not that I wanted to argue. The truth of it just hit me one day. After that I told him to take what he wanted. If there was anything I wanted after he was done I would take it. The only things I ended up taking were my clothes, my personal belongings and anything my parents had given me before their passing.

The large room was comfortable with an oversized rocking chair. An old sofa that has withstood the test of time to look perfect in this old setting and not look worn. An oversized chair. Small end tables sat next to each seat. Lamps were the only lighting. An island in the kitchen was perfect to sit at and to eat with an overhang all around for legs to slide under when sitting on the handmade stools.   That was probably built long before calling it an 'island' was a thing. I know there was, or used to be, a trap door under the island. Though this island is not the one that was there originally. When I was little the island was more like a table on wheels, with shelves under it. You could see the door with it's big iron ring to grab and pull the door up out of the floor on its hinges. It led to a cellar. As a child I had an aversion to going there even though Grandad assured me it was okay.   He told me his granddaddy had dug the hole himself. All I could picture was a big dirt hole. I did not like it so I never did go down there.

The warmth of the wood walls, aged and discolored from the sun was all the decoration the room needed.   I didn't hang any art or pictures. The kitchen that stretched along the back wall was lit beautifully from the long window that let light in and gave me a framed panoramic view of the mountains. I will never have to change this for the seasons, my display will change automatically.

I sat in the rocking chair. Between my job and my home I have been busy. Busy enough to always have something to look forward to and to keep me weary enough to sleep well at night. But today I crossed the last 'must do' off my list.

Tomorrow will be less busy.

Less busy with the must-do's but hopefully more busy with the get-to-do's. As I rocked slowly it came to me. I feel settled. I feel comfortable. I am happy.

II.

Waking up on a weekend day with nothing scheduled is new to me here. But I'm taking advantage. A slow drink of coffee with a buttered chunk of wheat bread I baked myself. I didn't make it. I bought frozen bread dough and baked it. The smell of it baking was enticing enough to make me want to bake it from scratch.

Between the information from my nearest neighbors, the internet and voyages to towns for groceries and house repair supplies I was learning the area. It was refreshing to come to small towns that still had hardware stores, book stores, butchers and bakeries. I got in the truck and took my half mile lane to turn onto the main road. My neighbors kept warning me to not be fooled by the nicely paved road. Come winter it will be a nightmare. I made my way down the mountain to the little village, where I did most hardware and grocery shopping. They also had an animal shelter that served a very large area. I had been considering getting a dog but wasn't yet convinced I should. I wasn't reeling as much from the divorce now and knew I wasn't looking for a relationship. But the idea of someone being around, and a dog counted as someone, was starting to feel right.

I'd never had a dog. Never thought much about getting a dog. I never thought it would be fair to acquire a dog just to leave it when I worked or traveled. Now that I could work more from home and traveling was not in my near future I have been thinking about it more often. I just wasn't sure about the commitment.

The animal shelter was closed when I drove past so I headed out of the village to the next town. It had a decent size book store.   Though I wasn't a dedicated reader I had decided to look into some books about mountain living, both for entertainment value and for information.   Living alone and quietly was new to me.   How did others do it. And why. I was more intrigued by the mountains every day.

The book store was open. The first books I saw were books by locals and books about local history. Considering the size of the town the book store was pretty large.   And diverse. I left with a used and old Betty Crocker cookbook because of the bread recipes and clear instructions.   Another book was about the local history.   Lastly, a book written about a local mountain man and his legend 'in these parts'.

I stopped to get some fresh vegetables after I left the book store and headed back to the animal shelter. They were open. I went in to talk with the young woman in the office. She gave me a good talking to about adopting a dog and their expectations. She gave me forms to complete, I did and handed them back. I spent quite a bit of time with her. She was patient and answered a lot of questions. She told me she appreciated me trying to become informed before getting a dog. She also gave me a list of things I might need to get, and consider, before I got a dog. She advised me not to buy food until I met my dog and knew what kind of food it would need. Knowing I wasn't ready to get a dog yet I didn't go meet any of the dogs they had in the back. I wanted to be as prepared as possible.

I stopped at my mailbox and with the mail found a flyer for a last minute get together tonight, a little ways up the mountain. Bonfire. Bring your own booze. Hotdogs and s'mores will be provided. It has been a nice distraction meeting the neighbors and slowly becoming acquainted with and part of the community. Gatherings have been informal, comfortable. Help and assistance have been offered. When I moved here I nearly anticipated becoming a recluse. But meeting these people has been a God send.

At home I scouted out where I would want the dog bed, food and water bowls. I looked online for the things I wanted to buy but knew I would try to buy it local first.

By dark I was loading a fresh baked (not home made) apple pie into the truck, a chair and a small cooler of beer. I dressed as warm as possible. I pulled into what looked exactly like what one would think a party on a mountain would look like. Random trucks, ATV's and jeeps parked off the sides of the lane leading to what looked like a building on fire, the bonfire was so big. People weren't standing too close to the fire. You could feel the heat before you got anywhere near it. Tables were set up with food covering them from one end to the other. Random coolers were sitting at the far end of the tables. I added my pie to the table and my cooler to the gathering of coolers. Some marked 'water', some marked 'pop' and the ones not marked were all going to be alcohol. A table set closer to the fire had hotdogs and sticks to cook them, and s'more fixings.

I stood a little transfixed by the fire. A lot transfixed. It was taller than the house that sat further back and higher up then where we stood. The clearing here was probably the largest cleared area I'd seen of any of the neighbor's yards. It was a beautiful old place. Like my place, it had been in the family for generations. Every generation had added something to the house. I'd been in it and was stunned at the depth of the house and the workmanship. All done by hands of the same family. The children in this house could touch the work of their great-great-grandparents. What treasure.

"Excuse me." I looked next to me where a young boy stood back with a plate of cookies.   I smiled.   He smiled.   "Mama told me to walk these around and offer them to folks. Want one?" I took a cookie as I was saying thank you and he hustled right off to the next person he could find.

The night was pleasant.   When I mentioned the possibility of getting a dog everyone had something to say. Some were pro-rescue-dogs all the way. Others said to think about what kind of breed I wanted.   Dogs were different and had different traits to consider.   This opened a discussion on rescue vs. purchasing bred dogs. It was enjoyable to listen to the pros and cons of both. It didn't turn into an argument.   It was pure discussion.   One thing everyone agreed on was you have to take very seriously the commitment to taking care of a dog.   They (the dogs) deserve it. Many offered up tips on housebreaking a dog if I got a puppy (highly recommended by many). Many suggested that a new to me, but older dog, may have some struggles adapting and I should not assume even if it is housebroke that it will maintain that in a new environment (strongly suggested by others). Everyone had something to say about how to feed a dog.

By the time I got home I was seriously doubting my ability to care for a dog. After all of the information shared and discussed I didn't think I was smart enough to have a dog.

When I woke up Sunday there was a covering of snow on the ground and flurries flying about. I spent the morning reading the book about the Mountain Man I had picked up yesterday. It didn't take much to put myself in the setting of the story. Not much of the area had changed since he died almost one hundred years ago. There was a map of the area that it turns out he was part of creating because of his knowledge of the mountain and its families. Properties that were owned by generations of family were still in many of those family names as I discovered while learning about them and the mountain. My own family name was written in neat print on the map, on the corner of the property where I now sat. It felt good to see that. Made me feel like I belonged.

I stopped reading long enough to make a meatloaf and put it in the oven. I checked the weather and decided if I was going to get into the office I better go tomorrow. After tomorrow it looked like it would be a little dicey.

As I stood at the kitchen counter cleaning up the makings of the meatloaf I stared out the window. The sky was grey. One large mass of clouds. No more snow flurries but they were coming soon. I thought of the days when I wouldn't be able to leave. I had an ATV in the garage, a used one I purchased after seeing how handy they came in up here. I used it a good bit to drag trees and branches when I started my cleanup. It would be nice if I had to get somewhere and didn't want to take the truck. I thought about being here and not being able to leave. How nice it would be to have a dog. I turned and leaned back on the counter, imagining a dog laying on its bed close to the wood burner. I slapped the dishtowel down on the counter. That's it.

I'm getting a dog.

By morning I had created the perfect dog in my head and how perfectly he would fit into my life. Now I have to meet him.

I went to work and did everything I could to be prepared to work from home for weeks if that's what it took. Others seemed to be of the same mind. Home office supplies were being restocked. Everywhere I looked people had copy-paper boxes on their desks filling them with files, sticky notes and pens. IT was busy with everyone's requests for updates on their laptops and making sure they would be connected and some needed VPNs installed.

I clocked out early and headed closer to home. I stopped at the general store in the village and was happy to find some dog bowls and a dog bed. I thought I should get food but remembered what the lady told me at the shelter. I better wait and see who comes home with me.

On the way home the shelter called to say my application was approved. They were getting ready to close and I was closer to home than the village so we agreed I would come in next week if possible.

At home I put my office/work things away and headed back outside. The sky was heavy and seemed to nearly meet the earth. Giving an enclosed feeling. The air was sharp in my nose, giving that tingly freezing feeling. I walked around, as I had developed a habit of doing, to pick up fallen or blown in sticks and branches. I deposited them in a corner of the wood shed.

Behind the house I stood staring at the mountains. Vividly I could recall granddad and dad doing the same. Just standing with the world. I closed my eyes and imagined them standing here. Close by. Three generations. It happened. We did stand here. Together. I'd like to think we still were.

I opened my eyes to see a snowflake falling gently to the ground. I've been here before. As a child, and an almost adult, in the snow. But I was never the one taking care of things. Granddad. Then dad. I never knew the level of work that went into being here. I had always just enjoyed being here.

The mountains had that blue hue, with grays and greens swooping around in layers. The peaks of the highest mountains I could see were capped in white. Though cold and getting colder I felt at ease and comfortable standing here. Knowing everything I need is in my home behind me. I wondered around to the workshop Grandad and his dad had built. Built to protect all of their tools and supplies against the elements and to have a place to work when the weather didn't want you outside. I went in and rummaged through some boards stacked on the 'wood shelves' at the back. I found what I needed and used the drill and screws that have long been here to make myself a bench. Nothing fancy but it felt sturdy enough. I took it back to where I had been standing behind the house and set it there.

Then sat on it a few more minutes just to test it out. Perfect.

Back inside I warmed up some meatloaf on the stove top, frying it, and made a thick sandwich. Along with some cut carrots, radishes and celery it was a fine little dinner. I put the kettle on the wood burner top and started the fire I should have started when I got home. It was dark outside and inside I didn't need much light. I kept a small light on by the big chair. A small light on the kitchen counter. The room was softly orange with the glow of fire through the door of the wood burner. With the mountains outlining the dark sky I couldn't imagine a more tranquil and restful setting.

I was lying in bed reading by 8 pm. It was still very new to me. Not working my life and my schedule around someone else.   Having the ability to rest, do nothing, or go non-stop all day, was a freedom.   Not necessarily a freedom I had wanted. But I was adjusting to it. Better than I initially thought I could or would. I didn't want to dwell on where he was or what he was doing. He had cut ties completely.   I don't know if he stayed in the condo or sold it. I don't know if he was alone or not. I don't know if he was working or not. I just know that having spent 17 years with another human being, and then without warning, there was nothing between you, had been a shock to the system.   We met in junior high, started dating in high school, married during college. We grew up together. Then we stopped growing together.   My brain had gradually accepted that here, and like this, is how I would be living... My heart was adjusting nicely as well. I couldn't imagine not being here right now. Wherever he is I hope he is well. But that's the limit of how much time I want to spend thinking about him.

I woke before the alarm. This happened more often than not since I moved here. I went to the kitchen and saw even in the dark morning that the world had been transformed. Quiet was my world. Snow had covered everything and covered it well. With snow comes the silence of a sleeping earth. I found the snow and the silence made it feel other-worldly. In a very good way.

I started the coffee and went outside to shovel the porch and a path to the lane that I wouldn't be driving out of anytime soon. I still had plenty of time to sit with my coffee and a piece of toast. There was no sunrise to see through the still hanging clouds.

Between video interviews, a couple of meetings and a lot of typing I put in a full day and then some. The perks of working from home were many as far as I was concerned. First and foremost was that I had my own private bathroom. Always. Second, at the end of the day I turned off my computer, turned off my desk lamp, walked out of the room, closed the door and my commute is complete. Comfort in my surroundings was something I had come to appreciate. How did work become synonymous with 'you can't be happy and comfortable while you work'.

A perfect day for stew. Once I commuted from work to my kitchen I browned some stew meat and chopped the vegetables. Quicker than I ever would have bothered before I moved here I had a pot of stew simmering on the back of the wood burner. I was getting much more comfortable doing this kind of cooking. Though I saw my parents and grandparents do this it had felt like a 'vacation' thing to do. A holiday thing to do. Not a regular living kind of thing to do. I was still adjusting, coming to understand that living here meant I could do all the things that I saw my parents and grandparents do.

I shoveled some more snow knowing I couldn't really keep up with it. But it would be easier to do every few hours or so than waiting and trying to do anything after it stopped. At least for now I felt I could keep doing this. Back inside, looking out the kitchen window I couldn't even see the bench I had just made and set out yesterday.

I finally sat down to some stew. I set my computer up so I could watch some Youtube videos but checked some news first.   Local news. Weather. It's snowing and it's going to snow some more was the jest of the weather.

A couple of the neighbors had sent texts checking on me.

Though I have been preparing for this. It was real now. I am snowed in.   Alone.   On a mountain.   As dramatic as this could and probably should sound I chuckled at the reality of it and the image of it while feeling safe and content instead of worried.

My phone ringing brought me out of my reverie. "Hello..."

"Hello, is this Aada?"

"It is."

"This is Bev from the animal shelter. I hope it's okay that I've called you."

"It is, of course. How can I help you?"

"Well, I think I've found a dog for you. But it's not through the shelter. I mean, it kind of is, but isn't."

"Oh, well sounds like there's a story with this."

"Just a little one. My cousin has a dog that they need to re-home. No problems with the dog mind you, it's family issues that I can't really explain. He isn't much more than a puppy. But he's a big-little fella. When my cousin was asking for my help I thought of you. Are you interested in knowing more?"

"I am."

"He's a Bernese Mountain Dog". As I was still sitting at my computer I searched the breed while she spoke. "He's going to get pretty big. He has all of his shots, he's the sweetest dog ever. I wish I could take him but my husband has put the kibosh on any more dogs."

While she talked I was staring at images of this beautiful dog. I looked around the big room and suddenly, oddly, felt like I could see him here. She was telling me about the breed as I was looking information up. Bev was telling me the biggest problem I will likely have with this dog is his shedding. I made a mental note to get used to that and not let it get on my nerves. Being a bit of a neat freak, super shedding dogs weren't exactly what I was thinking about or considering.

"Aada I have to tell you that this would not be a free dog." That didn't surprise me as I was looking at the information in front of me on the computer. Bev hurried on before I could speak. "Please don't think I'm trying to sell you a dog. I tried to talk my cousin into giving the dog to a good home but he does have quite a bit of money into him. He will also come with food, his own bed and bowls, leash and collar, a supply of vitamins, his toys, his brush and pin brush and some other things". I glanced at the bed and bowls sitting on the floor between me and the big chair. "He is already established at our vet here in the village". She paused to see what I would have to say.

While she talked I had searched for how expensive Bernese Mountain dogs are. I nearly choked on my surprise.

"To be honest Bev I hadn't considered buying a dog, that's why I went to the shelter. I know there are fees to adopt but I'm pretty certain it wouldn't be anywhere close to the cost of a Bernese Mountain dog."

"You're right. So right. I just thought of you first. Like I said, this isn't a sales pitch I promise. I just wanted to give you the first option. And I told my cousin that I would ask people who I thought would be a good home. But I'm not helping him sell his dog, I'm helping him find a good home for his dog."

"Just out of curiosity how much is he asking." I couldn't deny I loved the look of these dogs.

"He's only asking for five hundred. When I say 'only' please understand I know that is a lot of money. But to be fair to him it is helping him get some of the money he's paid for the dog's food, toys, and everything else. This puppy was meant to be a family dog and was going to be very well cared for and spoiled. But anyway, thanks for talking with me. I called you first so I do have a couple of other people to call."

"I'm glad you did call. I'm looking at these dogs and have to admit I am tempted. I just hadn't considered spending that kind of money."

"I do understand Aada." We wrapped up our conversation and ended the call. I did some more research on the dog. What a beautiful animal. I wondered about the heat on the mountains during the summer. Not that there were long or overly brutal summers but it could get hot. I was sad to see they had relatively short life spans compared to some dog breeds. I also listed out the items Bev told me about, including dog food and then did a quick calculation with what these things would cost if I had purchased them. It added up to a tidy sum that I will likely have to spend no matter what kind of dog I would get. I looked at the images on my computer. God, what a handsome dog. As I was contemplating this my phone rang again, same number.

"Hi Bev". She chuckled.

"Hi Aada. So I told my cousin about our talk. He trusts me on who I'm recommending for his dog. When I told him it was just too much he wanted to know if he dropped the price to $425 if that would help." I looked at my list and I looked at the dog. I know without a doubt this was a good deal. I didn't like the idea of buying a dog but I couldn't explain why.

"Bev, I do think I'm interested. Very interested." I looked around me. Half seeing the dog watching me with his head cocked. Like 'what are you waiting for'.

Though I am technically snowed in doesn't mean everyone is. When I told Bev it would be some time before I could get out she laughed and said I didn't have to worry about it. She knew where I lived because of the address on the application not to mention that it was well known I had moved back from 'the city' to live 'on the family place'. Her cousin lives on the mountain and has a snow-quad. He would be bringing the dog to me. As soon as I was ready. We agreed on tomorrow after I clocked out of work and once we met I could arrange payment through him. Contact information was shared. I thanked Bev for thinking of me.

Before I hung up I asked, what is the dog's name.

"Ukko".

III.

The next morning flurries were still flying but I wasn't sure if it was snowing or if the wind was just blowing loose snow. I started the coffee and went outside to shovel the porch and walkway again. As I was walking back up the walk it occurred to me the dog would be coming outside to do it's business. From the walkway I shoveled a path to the far side of the house and then some, heading towards the woods. I cleared as much of a square of ground as I could. Though it wasn't really cleared, it was just moving enough snow so Ukko could have space to move around without sinking into the snow.

Work was busy. After work I took the new bowls and dog bed out to my truck so I could return them. I'm sure Ukko would like his own dishes and bed more than something new. I made some dinner. I found myself more excited then I would have expected. I had never related to 'dog people', be it friends or co-workers, because I had never had one.

I was walking back up on the porch when I heard the growl of an engine. It didn't take long for this snow tracker to come up my driveway. It was a snow mobile on steroids with an enclosed cab. I couldn't see into the cab well because of the darkness of the winter day and the lights on the snow mobile. When he finally stopped he was parked sideways to me. There, on the passenger side of the cab, was Ukko.

I didn't become a dog person that minute.

I became an Ukko person.

IV.

Slowly I rolled over on the bed. As quietly as I could I looked over the edge of the bed, just trying to peek over. It didn't matter. No matter how quiet I was. Or how stealth I think I'm being, he is ready for me. I swear he looked up at me and sighed. Maybe even grinned. I smiled at him.

"Ukko I am trying my hardest to keep your hair out of my bedroom. Why can't you stay in your bed?"

He tilted his head. I knew he had an answer. He just wanted to be near me. Ukko wasn't just going to be a big dog, he was already a big dog. He was already bigger than the size of the kind of dog I thought I would end up with fully grown, and he wasn't anywhere near fully grown. I had put his bed in the big room. Close enough to the stove to feel the warmth but far enough away he wouldn't be anywhere near it. He liked his bed. He went there every night when I went to bed. But he always ended up on the floor by my bed sometime after I would fall asleep. With tips from Bev and the internet and his previous owner I had spent our time together being firm with boundaries. Ukko responded well to everything. Except staying out of my room. I didn't want to close the door because of the heat. The only thing I could think of next was to use a baby gate to keep him out.

I got up and slipped on the boots I now kept at the front door to go out with Ukko in the mornings. I pulled on the big down filled coat I kept with the boots and we walked outside. Ukko led the way to the lane and down the trail the snow mobile had made the day he arrived. He made the same trip every morning. Not during the day or evenings, just the morning. I then followed him back to the side yard where he did his business. Then he romped in the clean snow behind the house. Not for too long. He would look over at me and I swear he took pity on my standing there in my big coat and untied boots and felt he needed to take me back inside.

He was a tidy dog. Considering he left enough hair everywhere he went that I could make a spare dog. But he didn't make a mess eating. He put his toys in one spot when he wasn't playing with them. And during the day he always laid on his bed, never the furniture. I don't know if that was previous training or his preference.

I had tried closing my office door when I was on video calls or in meetings. He would lay at the door and softly whimper. It didn't seem to bother anyone else but it made me feel horrible. I tried letting him in during the calls to see how he would act. He would lay contently at my side without making a sound. He seemed to understand to not make noise when I was actually talking or listening to others. When I wasn't on video calls if he heard a snow flake drop he would bark at it.

Once I knew he wouldn't leave or wander off I let him out during the day when I took a lunch break. He always came at my first call. Each afternoon after work we went out into the snow. Ukko was made for snow. Or snow was made for him. He loved it. He didn't mind plowing through it and often led the way expecting me to follow in any of his newly broken paths. Ukko had gone behind the house often enough that we had paths we could walk around to the bench. I had cleared it off. I would go sit and watch him play in the snow. But as much as he liked to play, he liked to sit and stare out at the mountains too. Or he was mimicking me. He would stare out then look back at me. "Beautiful site isn't it Ukko". He would sigh.

Our morning routine would continue by going inside, I would get him breakfast and then get myself some coffee and toast. I did some research and decided to try feeding him three times a day. He seemed to appreciate it. He came with a good supply of food but it was quickly apparent he would be a costly boy to feed. I swept twice a day and had read to brush him once a week.

The days had been grey since his arrival. I enjoyed the lighting outside during these grey days. Everything felt softer. More peaceful. We had seen deer prints but not caught sight of any.

I went out to the car and retrieved the dog bed I had purchased before getting Ukko. I put it in my office where he normally lay next to me during the video calls. I took his regular bed in and put it by my bed. He watched, curiously. He followed me to the office and sniffed around the new bed then went to the big room and watched me take his bed into my room. He followed. He took an edge of the bed in his mouth and started pulling it back out of the bedroom. I watched while he pulled it back to its spot and put it right where it had been.

When I went to bed he went to his bed and lay down like he had been doing.

In the morning I again rolled over quietly, sneaking to the edge of the bed to peek over. There he was. Content as ever. We made our way outside to the grey and white world. Ukko went to the lane and back. He made his trek to the side yard. I left around the front of the house and came around to the back. There, quite majestically, was a buck. He stood with his back to me, his head up, as if he too was looking at the mountain scene in grey sepia with a hint of blue. I didn't move. He didn't move. We both seemed to be suspended in time. Though the bark that soon came bounding up behind me kick started time. I put my hand down and said 'stop'. Surprisingly

Ukko stopped. The buck, ever so casually and gracefully, turned his head to look at us. No alarm in his actions or skittish movements. His look assured him he was safe but now he was bored with us having broken his moment. He tossed his head and took a bound and a leap and was off and gone.

Ukko was standing against me, I could feel his chest moving as he breathed. I was surprised he stopped when he did and more surprised he didn't chase the deer or bark at him.

As I became more familiar with Ukko I could read him like I could a person. Probably better than a person. People's actions and behaviors are often expressed in manners to hide something, or protect something, of themselves.

Ukko was just an honest dog with no hidden agendas.

One Saturday I got up, went through our morning routine. Came back inside and puttered about doing what I needed to do. After awhile I lay on the couch. For some reason just feeling exhausted. I fell asleep and slept soundly for a couple of hours. When I woke up I found Ukko sitting between the kitchen island and the back wall of the kitchen where I would normally stand to prepare my meals. I tried to pet him and he turned his head away from me. I tried again and he again turned his head from me.

"Ukko. What's wrong? Why are you so mad?" He turned his head to look at me and just stared. Like I had any right to ask that question. I do believe he knew exactly what I had said. He walked over to his empty food dish. I felt quite contrite as I apologized and got him his food. When I put his dish down, before he ate, he leaned his head against my leg. I was forgiven.

I reminded him as he ate that he could take some responsibility. He could have woken me up if he was hungry.

From the beginning Ukko liked to be close. When he first arrived and met me he was understandably cautious. While we carried his belongings in to the house he watched, almost too quietly. He 'met' me and allowed me to pet him. The man bringing him to me was wonderful, he stuck around to make sure Ukko was okay with me. I could tell he didn't want to lose Ukko. I didn't ask the story on why he had to lose him. But I could tell it was hard on him, he buried his face in Ukko's fur when he said goodbye. He turned quickly to leave but not before I saw the tears.   Ukko watched the snow mobile drive away and then looked at me. I dropped to my knees in the snow and told him I would be good to him. For him. We would be good for each other.   I promised him kindness.   I talked softly to him until he came over to me. Close. I ran my hand over his head and he leaned into me.   My time around dogs has been minimal. Never having lived with one I never really understood the ability to communicate with a dog. Until that moment.   Ukko was sad.   He was kind. He wasn't opposed to me. He was just sad.

From that moment on he was clearly with me.   He loved being close. If I sat on the couch or chair he most often came over and sat next to me with his head and upper body laying into my legs. Or on top of my feet. If I stretched out on the couch he would sit on the floor but put his head on the couch.

Our days had settled into a clear routine. Not being able, or really needing, to leave helped establish that routine. But after two weeks of my only human contact being by phone, text or video calls I thought we needed to get out. There had been some traffic on the road. I knew there had been a plow through once or twice but not needing to leave I hadn't bothered to try.

Ukko hadn't yet been in my truck but he was more than happy to prance about as I cleaned it off. Once I was ready it didn't take any convincing to get him in. Though he did look back at the house as we were heading down the lane.   I wondered if he was having a flashback to leaving his last home.

"Don't worry Ukko.   We're coming back."   With that said he turned to face forward and appeared eager for a trip.

I've driven in snow before.   Even on this road when I would visit in previous years.   Always being advised by my father or granddad on whether I should be coming up the mountain or not. But driving it now knowing this was going to be my winter norm was a test of my nerves.   The snow plow did a great job of creating a visual barrier on the side of the road.   Guard rails, for some unknown reason, were few and far between up here.   So the snow gave a false sense of security.   What little space there was between the road and the drop-offs were piled high with snow. Though in some places it had fallen off and there wasn't even the false sense of security with a snow pile. Not that the entire road was along the side of the mountain or near drop-offs. But enough of it was that it could be frightening to think of sliding.

Taking my time and with Ukko keeping an eye out for anything he needed me to pay attention to with a soft bark we made it to the village safely and with relative ease. I picked up mail and packages at the post office. Including an enormous order of food for Ukko. I had hoped to buy it local but when I had contacted his veterinarian they had suggested the best way to get it was to order it myself. It would cost more if they had to order it for me.

Ukko sat patiently in the truck for me but I could tell he was watching every step I took. When I glanced out at him from inside the post office he was standing on the seat with his eyes attached to the post office. He saw me through the window and barked, sat on his haunches and waited. I had the two bowls I purchased behind my seat and as I pulled into the store parking lot to return them it occurred to me to keep them in the truck for when we are out. I got out and poured some water in one dish to see if Ukko wanted a drink. He did. Truck dishes for Ukko.

I enjoyed seeing people. During and after the divorce I had found myself becoming more private. Close to becoming, and willing to be, reclusive. It was almost a relief to not have to be around people constantly. The hard part about it was that it came at a cost I didn't make the decision to pay. The decision was made for me and I had to deal with the fallout. The comfort and interaction with people today felt refreshing.

I wanted to see how Ukko would do on a lead, or a leash. I went to the edge of the village and snapped a leash on to his collar. "Look Ukko. I want to go for a walk with you. There might be cars, or kids, or other dogs that I don't want scaring you. Or you scaring them. Let's see how we do with this okay?" We left the truck and walked the length of the street. I don't know what I was worried about. Ukko was a perfect gentleman. Even his barks seemed to be more "hello" than "I'm a dog and I'm here to bark at you". Ukko walked close enough to me that with every step his fur was rubbing my leg. If I tried to step over a little bit to give him more room he moved over a little bit to maintain that contact.

I'm pretty sure Ukko liked me.

And it didn't take long to see how much others liked Ukko. The majority of people we passed spoke directly to him, asked if they could pet him, or asked me about him. Ukko, though polite, was reserved. We only encountered one child. A small little guy. I kept my hand on Ukko's head, assuring him, while the little one stared at almost eye level with Ukko, Ukko being taller. Ukko looked at me. I gently took the child's hand with his father's permission and guided it to pet Ukko. Ukko dropped his head so the little boy could pet him, and I think, to make the child less afraid. Before I knew what happened the little boy threw his arms around Ukko. Ukko laid his head on the boy's shoulder, hugging him in return.

When we walked away Ukko looked at me and I couldn't do anything but smile, impressed with his gentleness.

It was an enjoyable afternoon. I walked by one cafe and saw a small sign that said 'pet friendly' but it appeared very full inside. I suspect a lot of people were taking advantage and getting out today. It was still grey but it hadn't snowed in over a week. The road crews were getting a chance to clear more roads. And people were just tired of 'having' to stay home.

I walked Ukko back to the truck. I got him some more water and treats before we got back in. I stopped at the grocery store and realized this would be the longest time away from him since he came to me. "Ukko, just wait here. I won't be long. I have your food in the back and I need a few things for me. Okay?" I put my hand on his neck and gave him a 'good boy' rub. When I came back Ukko sat in the passenger seat looking straight ahead. I got in after putting my groceries next to his food in the truck bed, locking the bed cover. He never once turned to look at me. I think I need to get him used to not being with me 24/7. Or get him to understand I have to step away from him sometimes.

By the time we got home it was already getting dark and he had forgiven me. I let him go about his business and play in the yard while I took everything into the house. I went on the porch when I finished, watching him. I was mildly surprised at how quickly I got used to having Ukko around. Prior to moving here I would never have spent this much time at home, or alone. When I was married we were on the go. We went to work, we went out to eat, we went to parties, we went on trips, we just went. Looking back it was easy to say we were avoiding being alone. But there was a time when we were just having fun, a lot of fun. But I wouldn't go back to that now. Even if it meant my marriage wouldn't have ended in divorce. I watched Ukko. He seemed to like it here. I always did like it here. It wasn't until I moved here that I came to appreciate it like Granddad and dad must have.

This was feeling like home in a way I hadn't felt since leaving my parents home and going to college.

Ukko was rolling in the snow.

I was leaning against one of the porch roof posts.

The night was grey but it wasn't so dark you couldn't see. There were no stars. The clouds appeared to remain immoveable as they had been for two weeks.

I turned to go in, deciding to see what Ukko would do without me calling him. By the time I took the few steps to reach the door he was right behind me. I was beginning to understand that even when Ukko didn't appear to be paying attention, he was always paying attention.

Over the next couple of days I had made plans for two different friends to come visit on the weekend. Depending on the snow. Both had been here during the first month I was here full-time, neither had been here since then. I had gone to see each of them as well. I knew when I moved here that relationships were going to change. No longer being in people's immediate circles usually, not always, made things change. I already felt the changes. I was okay with it and I had started to make new friends here. I prepared myself to feel lonely but wasn't surprised when I didn't. I was too busy working on establishing myself in my job and in my home. Not to mention I was healing. Though coming out of it all I surprised myself with starting to feel more comfortable and happy then I could remember being in a very long time.

I hadn't anticipated that. I thought at the beginning of the divorce that I would always miss 'this'. Him. I was wrong.

Meeting up with my friends was something I enjoyed but not something I needed to do on a regular basis. Not since the divorce. I discovered how much I enjoy solitude. I liked my job well enough. Got along well with my co-workers and clients. Most importantly I feel like I am becoming part of this community. A community where your neighbor isn't a holler away over the fence or on the other side of a wall but a mile or ten over mountain roads. I was becoming a part of a world I didn't know I missed until I was here and realized I had missed not being part of it sooner.

The day after plans were made for both friends to visit we had a new layer of snow. About 12 inches worth. Except where it was blowing. There were drifts as tall as me. When I opened the door in the morning to go out with Ukko I would have sworn he shouted with glee as he took a leap and sailed off the porch into the snow. I couldn't help but laugh at his joy. It was also the first morning he didn't go down the lane. He just bounced and played in the snow. I wonder if that's a sign he trusts me, or knows this is his place.

I stood watching Ukko while sending texts to my friends. As quickly as we had scheduled visits we had to cancel.

I was as happy with this snow as Ukko. Not the discomfort or issues it caused for many. But snow, itself, is beautiful.   From where I stood I could have, in the minute, believed the whole world was in a snow globe. Encircled in the grey skies that touched the borders of the white snow.   Green of the pines.   Blacks and browns of the trees.   The world felt minimalistic as I stood in it. Basic. But fresh and clean. Powerful in its solitude.

I clocked in for work on time despite the snow. My supervisor enjoyed my snow pictures but reminded me that my commute from kitchen to office was pretty safe.   Many of my co-workers didn't live in or visit the mountains much. I think I won the video-meeting-snow-pictures display everyone was sharing when I disconnected my work computer from all of its scanners/printers/etc to take it outside and show them my view.   They greatly enjoyed Ukko taking full advantage of an unscheduled door opening to dash out and bounce around in the snow again and my attempts at getting him to come back in. He had never done that before. I am convinced he was showing off. When he came back in he looked at me and walked with head held high to his bed by the stove.

After work I FaceTimed with my two friends who had to cancel their visit because of the snow. I was sitting on the floor with my back to the couch. Ukko was at my side with his head in my lap. When I started talking to my friends he became very intrigued with the laughter and the conversation. At first he remained still, then his head would tilt up. He knew this was different than the day time video calls when he sat calmly in the office. Before the call was over he was sitting next to me with his head next to my head, fully engaged in the conversation. Invested in the reactions. Or something. He brought a level of entertainment that I wasn't capable of. Just by sitting there watching them. Whenever someone said his name he gave a short little bark of acknowledgment.

When we hung up I looked at him and asked him if he understood us. He yipped and vibrated his head as he looked up. "You're brilliant Ukko".

We were sitting in near dark but for the glow of the fire and one of the small lamps I had on. I don't know how Ukko felt but to me it was very insulating, in a good way. Warm. Cozy and secure feeling all at once.

I went to the kitchen and discovered the clouds had broken. There was a patch of dark sky with brilliant stars and the moon. Inexplicably I was so overcome with a wave of emotion my hand went to my chest as if I could physically grab that feeling. Sadness? No. Not at all. Just ... emotion. Without me having said a word or made a sound Ukko was by my side, pushing his head into me. I looked at him. I lay my hand on his head as he lay his comforting weight against my leg. The darkness outside permitted visibility. I could see the mountains. The trees, dark in the night. The snow, all shades of brilliant white and blue grey, as the shadows played softly on the surface. Everything I could see somehow felt palpable, as if I could feel the beauty and depth of it. Ukko and I were alone with this world, this vision, tonight.

I don't know how long Ukko and I stood there like that. Me needing to absorb the visual and the emotion of something so stunning. But not really being able to take it all in without Ukko's presence and connection. How grateful I am to be living this moment, on this mountain, with this amazing creature.

V.

I started to add afternoon walks, after work, to our routine. We both needed it. One day we would go up the mountain road. The next day we would go down the mountain road. Once or twice a week we would take one of the paths I used to take with Dad or Granddad. The snow wasn't going anywhere any time soon. I kept the paths around the house and side yard cleared for me and Ukko. Ukko would plow through other paths for me to follow. After one of our walks a neighbor showed up and used her snowblower to clean off my lane. She let me give it a go and when I went back in the house I put it on my 'wish list' deciding it would be a great Christmas gift for me and Ukko. She also let me know about a get together at the old Foster Farm. While talking with me she was petting Ukko and said "bring him, everyone will love him".

I hadn't thought of the Foster Farm since I'd been here with Granddad. He was friends with them. They had pig roasts in the fall, Christmas parties, and 'spring flings'. I always thought they were rich. Granddad told me they were rich, but not like how I thought. He told me they were rich in friendships and family. They were "lovely people" who enjoyed seeing others happy. The Foster Farm was still occupied by Foster descendants.

I decided to take the ATV. I put Ukko in front of me between my arms and my legs. As bundled up as I was I don't think I would have survived that ride if not for Ukko's body. He faced the wind of the ride and loved every minute of it.

The night we returned from the Foster Farm get together both Ukko and I were exhausted. A lot of people, a lot of dogs, a lot of stimulation that neither of us were used to. But I'm pretty sure Ukko enjoyed it as much as I did. I'm pretty sure Ukko was passed out before me. Tromping in snow was exhausting.

I woke with a caution feeling. Ukko was standing next to my bed. He never does that. He was looking at my bedroom window. He wasn't quite tall enough to see through it as the bedroom windows were higher than the other windows in the house. I started to move and Ukko made a noise, not a bark or growl, but I swear he was telling me to be quiet. Cautiously I got up and slowly started to stand tall enough to look out the window. If something was out there I didn't want it to see me but I sure wanted to see it.

As I got my eyes clear of the window sill I saw something that I didn't quite register at first. On the edge of the clearing. I had a difficult time distinguishing it from the trees and the shadows. Until it moved.

I ducked down to Ukko and asked him "is that a moose?" I've heard tell of moose coming up this far in the mountains but I had never seen one. Granddad had told me how he would see them on occasion. But in this snow? How did he get up here through all the snow?

As quiet as I could I went to the kitchen with my phone. I wanted to take its picture. He was magnificent. I could get a better look at him through the kitchen windows. How big do moose get? Why is he here? He started to move closer toward the trees.   Into the trees.   And disappeared.

Ukko, who was standing quite tense, relaxed. "It's alright Ukko. He must just be passing through. But if you ever see one up close don't go up to them.   They can get pretty aggressive."   I hugged him and thanked him for being so alert and protective. When I went back to bed he walked into my room but was facing the outside wall like he was making sure nothing was out there. He seemed content and went back to his bed.

It being my first full winter I wasn't accustomed to the weather patterns yet. Or what seemed to be the lack of a pattern. There would be days of snow. Then days of isolation before I felt comfortable on the roads. Then one week, or two, of a warm up. Just as Ukko and I would begin to venture out, making trips to work or stores, we would get more snow again.

At the Foster Farm gathering some of the neighbors had decided to start a texting group for information/weather/dangers/concerns etc. There were about fifteen families, including myself, who added our numbers to the group. It was like a neighborhood watch. But a mountain sized one. It was created with the idea to be able to check on one another during storms and outages and to send out any concerns about roads, or information that roads were clear, etc. It turned out to be a saving grace on more than one occasion.

Not long after it was established a text went out asking how everyone was doing after yet another snowfall added another layer of snow. Even though we knew the additional snow was coming people sometimes get caught off guard. Was everyone safe? Did everyone have power/water/food. Everyone checked in but one neighbor, "Hammer", an older gentleman who lived alone. Numerous texts and phone calls were attempted. The nearest neighbor to him who had a snowmobile went to check on him. They found him unconscious in his house. His dogs were all lying around him keeping him warm. His fire had gone out. Rescue was arranged and they got him to the hospital. Through the text group it was arranged to foster his dogs, his house was closed up and checked on by the neighbor who found him. When the roads were clear Ukko and I were part of the 'team' of neighbors who went to visit him while he was in rehabilitation. He had known Granddad and Dad. I made a new friend. He made two. Ukko became very fond of him.

On one of our drivable days we went to the village for a veterinarian appointment for Ukko. Being completely clueless about having a dog I wanted to make sure of what Ukko needed. Research I did online assured me of some things, raised concerns or confusion for others. I did worry about Ukko come summer. He was a snow dog. And though summers on the mountain weren't long, they could get pretty hot. The vet was kind, and had already met Ukko. He gave Ukko a once over and felt his weight was perfect though I was shocked to learn he was over 100 pounds. I was doubly shocked to realize how tall he was. He was almost two and a half feet tall while standing on all four paws.   The vet said he was a 'big boy'.   Being with him every day I didn't quite notice the growth.

The vet asked if I had air conditioning at home. I did. He said Ukko would be fine in the summer if he has a place to be cool.   He suggested having a groomer for him but be aware if anyone tells me to thin or trim his body hair. The areas around his face and ears may need trimmed, he pulled up some sites online that he trusted and showed me some information and gave me the sites to go to for any tips and care advice. I felt much better when we left about being able to keep him healthy through any heat.

We walked around the village and this time the cafe with the 'pet friendly' sign was empty.   I opened the door against the cold and asked the girl wiping off the table if it was okay to bring Ukko in. She waved me in while saying 'of course'. Ukko and I took a table by the window. She came over and offered her hand, palm down, for Ukko to sniff. He did for a second before licking her. She dropped down to her knees and asked him if he wanted some water, he yipped. She took that as a yes. As she walked away to get him his water she turned back to me with a laugh and asked if I wanted anything, as an after thought. I replied a coffee with cream. I smiled. I didn't blame her a bit.

I can't speak for all dogs seeing as how Ukko is the only one I've known. But he is special. He's a personable fella. I know without any doubt that he understands me and probably most people. Walking in the village, or stopping at the rehab, people speak to him before me. Sometimes instead of me. Sometimes they talk to me by talking through Ukko.

The young girl brought a dog dish of water and a cup of coffee out to us. She lingered to pet Ukko but lingered longer to talk. She seemed bored, or lonely, or in need. I wasn't sure which. And it didn't matter. Sitting there, talking with her and watching her enjoy Ukko was an enjoyable break. It appeared she was the only one there, I was hungry, but didn't want to make her step away from Ukko or our table. I asked her to sit with him for a minute so I could look at the pastries and pies. I went up to see what was on offer and when I returned she was fully sitting on the floor with him. I went back to the counter asking as I went if I could just grab myself a pastry. She said 'sure' appearing quite content to not get up. I brought it back to the table. I took some treats out of my backpack and gave them to her for Ukko. She 'good-boy'ed him and treated him while I ate my pastry. When I knew I had to leave to get up the mountain before dark I handed her enough money for the bill and a tip.

The cafe and the young girl became a regular visit for Ukko and I on our trips to the village.

Winter lived on. Ukko felt more an extension of me sometimes then my own hand. He was close when I needed him to be close. He kept to himself when he knew I had to do things without him. He was intuitive. Gentle. I never knew how much I needed him. Not 'a' dog. Him.

One night I went outside. I couldn't sleep. I bundled up with a blanket and sat on the top step looking out at the white snow bordered with grey blue shadows. The moon was so much closer up here on the mountain than anywhere else I had lived. Or, I was more aware of it without the busyness of a city, it's buildings or people to obscure the viewing of it. I thought I got out of the cabin without waking Ukko up. I should have known better. I heard him snuffling at the door. I got up and let him out and sat back down. He sat next to me on that top step. Together we just sat. Looking at the stars. Or the snow. Or into the trees.

"Sorry Ukko, I didn't mean to wake you."

Head shake, no worries.

"I don't know why I can't sleep. I bet I'll be good and tired at 6:30 when the alarm goes off."

Head turn to look at me. Yup.

"Sometimes I wish I knew what you were thinking."

He put his paw on my shoulder. Then he dropped it next to me again and just leaned on me. With my heavy blanket and Ukko I wasn't cold. The night was so crisp. The air. The view. I've been on vacation before when I stood in a place and nearly held my breath at it's beauty and made very conscious efforts to be aware of everything, retain it, because I want to remember the feeling of being there. Now, I can come outside and do this all the time. But I still want to remember this minute. Sitting on the steps, with Ukko, and the moon, and the shadows, and the comfort of it all.

My first night here after the divorce, not just for a visit, but my first night of full time living here I did not know this feeling. Not all of it. There was familiarity to it, comfort in having it to come back to. Appreciation for my parents and grandparents who made this a place I would always love coming to without knowing I would be here full time. But that first night I was still somewhat in shock. I walked around. Touching things that had been here my entire life. There were some tears for missing those who had been here but no longer were. There were some tears for missing the life I thought I had wanted and then had no say in it ending. There were some tears for not knowing what was coming.

Also that night, the tears stopped. A plan started to form even if I wasn't fully certain of what that plan would entail. I knew this place was part of that plan.

I leaned my head on top of Ukko's head. Never would I have imagined, in my other life, that being here with a dog made me happier, content even, then any other part of my life to this point.

As predicted when the alarm did go off later that morning I was fast asleep. Instead of feeling groggy I woke feeling fresh as the morning itself. As I peeked over the edge of the bed there was Ukko looking as eager as ever to start the day.

V I.

I went on a date. It went okay. When I got home Ukko didn't play any games. He came up to me, smelled me, walked away acting a little bit indignant. It wasn't a date that would lead to other dates and it told me what I suspected. I wasn't ready. I wasn't looking. I'm quite happy with where I am in life.

Eventually the snow left. Though remnants of it stayed around for a very long time on the shadier parts of the mountain. Ukko and I went out and explored more. We went to the cafe one night a month for karaoke night. I never sang, out of respect for others, but we always had a good time. Our neighbor, Hammer, had returned from rehab so we would visit with him or he would stop by our place. After work I spent more time cleaning out the debris nature left in the woods. With all of the downed trees it would be a very long time before I would have to pay for firewood. I spent a lot of time cutting and hauling. Moving the older wood in the shed to the front and putting newer wood in the back.

Ukko and I went to an ATV store recommended by many of the neighbors. I wanted something we could ride on together but would also still be a tool to help with pulling trees and doing other work around the land. I was a little jealous of the snow tracker Ukko's first family had brought him to me in. I had researched until I was sure I could handle it financially and was fairly certain of what I wanted. I felt it was necessary enough to dip into my savings. We pulled the trailer with my first ATV to the store hoping to get a good trade-in deal. We pulled the trailer back home with a side by side ATV with a cab and a bed for hauling. After I got it unloaded, the trailer unhitched and put away, I couldn't find Ukko. I called for him and heard his yup reply. He was sitting in the passenger side of the ATV. We rode until dark. He was in shotgun seat heaven.

Ukko and I decided to go fishing. I hadn't been fishing since Granddad had died but I fondly remembered the lakes and ponds we had gone to. The shed still had the fishing poles and a very dusty tackle box. With all of the old gear and Ukko riding shotgun we went to our friend Hammer's house, doing well since he was home from rehab. He was a great help. The rod I wanted to use was in great shape though it needed new string. He thought the string had probably not been cast in a couple of decades. He kept the other

2 rods I took and said he would work on those for me. He looked through my tackle box and told me what was good and what wasn't and made some suggestions. He seemed to be having a great time and kept mentioning 'when' he used to fish. I asked if he wanted to come along. I didn't need to ask twice. He got his own, not used in way too long, gear. Packed himself and me a few beers and bologna sandwiches to go with my apples and peanut butter and jelly sandwiches. His dogs were older and he didn't want to tax them so he left them home. When we got into the ATV to head out fishing I was proud of Ukko as he jumped into the back without having to be coaxed.

What a great first day of fishing. We didn't catch anything but we had a great time. The first of many.

Hammer was a great story teller. I most enjoyed his stories of Granddad and Grandma, and his own stories of growing up on this mountain, getting married, his time in the service. All of it. I told him he should write a book. He 'pshaw'ed me. But I loved listening.

When we returned he invited me in for a dinner of chili he had made the day before. His dogs welcomed Ukko as the old friend he has become. We spent the evening looking at his photo albums, I even saw pictures of my grandparents. What a wonderful day. A day I wouldn't have had without the divorce. It occurred to me as I drove home that I have much to thank the divorce for. I reached over and ran my hand through Ukko's fur. Number one, right here.

Another night I couldn't sleep. These nights weren't as difficult as they once were. It wasn't stress or emotional turmoil that kept me awake or woke me in the middle of the night. I came to think of these nights as Gratitude Awakenings. I made my way to the front porch. I didn't even try to not wake Ukko, it wasn't possible. He came outside with me. It was pretty dark, it was raining, and it smelled so unbelievably sweet. I sat in the rocker. He lay on the rug I had put out there for him.

I rocked. He started to snore. It's been over a year since I've been living here. I never knew life could be like this. All the time. I'm more comfortable at home then I am going out. Rock, rock. When I do go out I see people who are part of life here. It's neighbors who check on you, lend a hand, or just know about you and are glad you're part of their world. Rock, rock. Friendships have taken on a new level of honesty and value. Some old friendships have gotten stronger. Some have quietly ended, no drama, just different directions. New friendships have started and are so diverse my life is richer than I ever knew it could be. Rock, rock. I don't feel a need to find a partner because something is missing. I don't feel like anything is missing, I am complete in myself. Rock, rock. I don't know emptiness. I couldn't help but reflect on the 17 years prior to moving here where another person, I thought, filled my life. And now I don't know anything about him. I wasn't curious. But I couldn't help reflect on how life changes. With or without your consent. Rock, rock, rock.

Towards the end of summer I had completely restocked the wood shed, and put even more wood in the tool shed. I had dragged logs and piled them on the far side of the wood shed for future cutting and chopping.

Hammer and I were going fishing about once a week or so and he promised to filet anything we caught because I had developed a dislike of fish guts. But I had to do the cooking. So at least once every two weeks we had fish fries.

Karaoke had turned into a nice social event. Ukko went with me. I innately trusted Ukko when it came to people. I knew when he liked someone and when he didn't. I didn't always know why he was wary of someone but it was enough of a red flag for me to say no to a date request. There were a couple of dates with different men that summer, all from karaoke night, and all with Ukko's approval. Still nothing that turned into romance. But some nice friendships started.

I took care of Ukko how I would want taken care of. I got him to the vet when he needed it. I pulled burs from his fur. I bought him the best food and treats I could get for him. But I was well aware it was Ukko helping lead me along. I trusted his instinct. I would like to think he trusted mine, though he didn't need it.

One day on the mountain we were walking an old familiar path for the first time since my childhood with Granddad. I was lost in the headiness of the oddly fragrant air. More so than I remembered ever smelling it. Ukko was walking ahead of me. It wasn't sweltering hot but for him it was probably hotter. I hadn't been here in some time but it was a favorite of Granddad's. The path was narrow enough that the tree branches met from both sides of the trail, over the trail, in many places. The earthy smell meeting the fragrance in the air was better than anything man could create.

It was not a well used path, all the shame for others, all the better for us. I knew we were close. I called for Ukko to stop. If he was a teenager I am certain his reaction was a dramatic sigh and an eye roll. When I got to him I took him by the collar which surprised him, and when I snapped on his leash he was confused. "Not safe Ukko". We breached the trees with just a few steps and with only a few more steps we were on the edge of a cliff. We stood on the precipice of the earth. It would seem.

Ukko shuffled back a couple of steps and dropped to his haunches. I stepped back and sat with him. "Didn't expect this did you boy?"

Before us was a panoramic view of earth. At least this part of it. The colors were brilliant. The air still so fragrant. The wind was stronger out here than on the path. The sun a little warmer. I pulled off my backpack and poured Ukko a drink of cool water. He was looking out past anything he'd seen before, even living on the mountain, this view wasn't anything like home's. He appeared mesmerized. I nudged him "drink Ukko". Ukko looked down at the water dish and back to me with surprise. "Drink Ukko". He drank.

Then he sat in his own majestic beauty existing within this majestic beauty.

"It's incredible isn't it?"

A yip and head shake.

Mountains, after mountains, and still more mountains, on the horizon. Blankets of trees rolling out embroidered with ribbons of water falls and crevices. Birds flying in front of us, below us.

That day, that place, became our favorite place together.

Autumn came soon enough. I was so grateful when the air turned a little cooler. Ukko loved being outside. He didn't act like the heat bothered him but it worried me when he wore the equivalent of a bear suit year round.

I readied for winter. Our trips to the village and the next town always had an extra errand to get more to stock up on. I went to the office a little more often knowing the days would be fewer and farther between once the snow hits.

We made sure Hammer and his dogs were well supplied. I lectured Hammer, maybe a little too much, about keeping his cell phone charged and with him always. He was well stocked with wood. The neighbor who had rescued him last year had convinced him to get a full house generator. We all felt better when that was installed and ready to use if he needed it.

The text group was filling up with advice and warnings. A heavy rain was coming, and the temperatures were dropping.   We didn't have to worry about snow we had to worry about ice.

And we got it. I salted the porch and steps when the temperature dropped. Ukko and I slept through the night. The rain. The freezing. The crystallization of our world. When I opened the door to go out with Ukko, the world was frozen in icicles and sheets of shimmering, glittering blue, white, grey ice. The trees sparkled as if made of silver. A new sound greeted us. I could hear cracking and snapping as soon as we came out. Branches and trees couldn't bear the weight of this ice. The sounds were echoing throughout the mountains.   It added to the sensation of stepping into a different world. Ukko didn't know what to make of it. I had put some crampons I found in the shed on my boots the night before. Ukko knew something was different. But he wasn't sure what.

He took to the steps before I could get there to warn him. The steps weren't frozen because of the salt and the cover of the porch roof. But when he stepped down from the steps and hit that frozen ice covered ground he slid and spun and sputtered and yipped. I tried to say his name to calm him but couldn't stop laughing. Gingerly, not sure if I could trust the studs on the shoes in the ice, I stepped off the porch to get to him. He kept pawing at the ice trying to get on his feet and continued to spin and move. I kept trying to get to him. He kept yipping. I kept laughing.

I had to stop because I was out of breath from laughing. When I stopped, he stopped. Looking a little indignant. He was splayed out on the ice. "Ukko. Don't move. Just stay there and let me come to you. It's ice buddy. It's brand new to you." He started to move again. "No Ukko. Stay." I finally made my way to him and lifted him on to his feet. Damn he was heavy. I held on to his collar. He was yipping like a puppy. I kept hold of his collar and we made it around to the side of the house closest to the woods. I walked him up to the woods hoping the ice hadn't gotten through the trees as bad. When we walked through the trees and got into the dense woods he could feel the earth again. Though the trees were a little concerning with the branches hanging under the very heavy weight of the ice. I let him go and he sniffed around the ground and found it familiar enough to do his business.

Though I was concerned about the branches, standing under a frozen canopy of trees was stunning.

Ukko was avoiding going back on the ice. I had to coax him, take him by the collar and walk him back to the house. How do you explain to your dog that the yard is an ice rink. For the rest of the day he would go to the door and look out. He would go out on the porch and lie down but not risk going down the steps. Before starting work for the day I took a load of salt and spread it on the same path we took up into the woods. He wouldn't go out at lunch time. After work I took him back out. He lay on the porch. I had to coax him down the steps and take him by the collar. We went back to the woods again. I took an old ax with me. He noticed the difference in the ice where the salt had pitted it. I used the ax to chop up any smooth places to give us some traction. When we headed back to the house I let go of his collar and let him navigate on his own. While he lay on the porch I took the snow shovel and knocked off icicles and any ice I could reach around the edges of the roof.

As soon as I stepped back inside the house the power went out. Ukko noticed the difference and looked at me like I had performed a magic trick. "The electric is out Ukko". My phone started pinging with messages with everyone checking in to see if everyone else lost power too. Everyone had. I was pleased to see Hammer responding. Everyone was safe.

My generator was already kicking on. There was no telling how long

the electric would be out. I made
sure my portable battery packs were
fully charged. I lectured Ukko all
through the day about how this
could impact us. He seemed to
agree. I brought more wood in.
Ukko opted to just hang out on the
porch. He was loving the
temperature but still not a fan of the
ice. When he did come in he sat with
me on the floor as I leaned up
against the couch when I video
called with some friends. He had
met some of them and I could tell
who he liked and who he was bored
with.

The first few days, even with work, I
kept busy with baking bread.
Cookies. I even made some dog
treats I had been wanting to try
making. I made stew. I made chili. I
made pasta with tomatoes, onions,
garlic and feta cheese. I now had a

fridge and freezer full of left over foods.

Ukko got more comfortable with the ice and would take his path up to the woods and hang out up there or on the porch. The cracking of the trees was still pretty bad. There was no sun. The temperatures weren't rising. We were sealed in a frozen ice ball.

My laundry was hanging all over the living room to dry. The dryer was working but I didn't know how long I would be without power and conserving energy was a good idea.

I sat on the couch facing the kitchen. I needed to do something. I didn't feel like risking a broken leg by going outside. But I couldn't just sit here any longer. I had contemplated redoing the kitchen island. I felt if I made it more open like Granddad's original island, with open shelves underneath, it would make the room feel even lighter. I'm not sure what happened to the cellar. In my mind I had always considered it as having been filled in and sealed off. I am pretty sure that's what dad said when I came for a visit with Grandad and mom and dad and saw the new island. I wonder if the floor was replaced or the island just built over the opening or trap door. It was appealing to think of seeing that trap door with that big old iron ring again.

I went to the island and got on my hands and knees to see if I could tell if the floor had been replaced where the trap door had been. I couldn't tell. But was very surprised to see that the island was on tracks. I looked up under the overhang and saw a small lever. I hooked my finger in it and pulled, the island slid open. What appeared to be the framing of the island stayed in place while the cabinet piece moved, exposing an open hole.

I scuttled up and over to the flashlight hanging in the utility room and went back.

I shined the light in the hole.

What the hell.

The cellar had not been closed off or filled in. The hole was still there with an opening, with stairs, to the cellar. But it was more than just the cellar I thought I remembered. In my recollections it was a dark pit.

What the actual hell.

I lay on the floor and shined the light down, surprised at what I was seeing. Ukko was looking with me. I looked at him, he looked at the hole, and when I jumped up excited he got excited. I took the flashlight and maneuvered onto the step. Ukko barked at me as I stepped further down but he didn't follow. He barked at me. "It's okay Ukko. Come Ukko." He stayed where he was, barking. I stood at the bottom of the steps. They were made out of rough hewn wood but solid and aged. I shone the light around and was excited. The room was small but finished. The walls were very similar to the walls upstairs, the same kind of wood. There was a very old, very large, arm chair with an ottoman. Behind the chair were shelves made out of the same rough hewn wood as the stairs. They were full of books. I was surprised to see a lamp sitting on a rough made small table by the chair. What are the chances? I went to it and turned the switch, it did not turn on. I looked into the shade, it wasn't plugged in and no bulb. The room was maybe 14' by 14' or a little bigger. There were some cabinets built halfway up one wall, the top of the cabinets had a plank of wood, like a shelf, with candles and other odds and ends sitting there, like a mantle. In the middle of the mantle was a large iron ring attached to a square of wood from a very familiar floor. It was the original ring for the trap door.

As I spun and took in the room I was excited. It was like a time capsule. Under the steps was more shelving. With canned foods! I went over and found empty jars stacked neatly. On the lower, taller shelves, were heavy earthenware crocks. Some with lids

made from wood. I saw that most of
the glass jars were actually empty
but there were some that appeared
to have green beans in them. Green
beans I would not be eating.

The floor was made of the same wood
as the floor upstairs.

I went to the shelves with the books,
there was a small framed picture of
me, one of my parents, one of my
grandparents, one of Granddad with
his father, standing very proper, in
front of this cabin.

Ukko was still barking. "Ukko,
come." He wouldn't. I went upstairs
to find a lightbulb. I came back down
and put it in the lamp, plugged it in.
Turned it on. It worked. The lamp
was old but those old lamps are
pretty indestructible. When I got the
light on I went back to the bottom of

the steps. "Ukko, come. You'll like it. I promise." He pranced around not sure how to get on the first step. I waited. He finally figured it out.

He stopped next to me and looked around. He cautiously sniffed the entire room. Especially the chair. He circled the chair three times. Finally, he jumped up on the chair and sat there. I had never seen him jump on a piece of furniture. I couldn't reprimand him. I had never told him to stay off of the furniture. He just did. Apparently he is claiming ownership of this chair.
How did I not know about this room? Why was it closed off?

I sat on the ottoman at the foot of the chair.

The room was dry. Comfortable. An old smell but not a bad smell.

The book shelves were full. I pulled out a book. "All Creatures Great and Small" by James Herriot. I opened the cover. In Granddad's writing, his name, the year "1975" and "I loved it!". I pulled out other books. They all had his name, a year, and a brief description of whether he liked it or not. I assumed the year was the year he read it. I put all of the books back but held onto "All Creatures Great and Small". It felt like a treasure. The room. The books. His handwriting.

I just sat and stared. How did I not know this room was here. I knew there was a cellar but I don't know that I ever knew it to be more than basically a dirt floored cellar. How could I have forgotten it? Did my parents use it? It started to make me feel a little guilty. That I hadn't been here enough to know or remember it.

Ukko was oddly comfortable considering he was so hesitant to come down here. He lay with his head on his paws. The chair was big enough to hold his largeness with comfort. I was happily shocked. I lay my hand on his head. "Ukko, why would anyone just close up this room? Why wouldn't dad or granddad tell me about it?" Ukko didn't know either apparently.

I went to the cabinets. They weren't very deep but ran almost the length of one wall. I sat in front of the first set of double doors and opened it. Inside were old albums. The kind with heavy black construction paper as pages. The pictures were held by little paper corners glued to the page. I carefully pulled one of the albums out.   It was in good shape. The age I understood it would have to be made me handle it gingerly. Inside were very old photographs. Faces looked back at me that I was not familiar with.   They had to be family. Right? Why else would they be down here in this time capsule. Most of the people were posed in rigid stances. Typical of the first era of photography. In one album I could see this very cabin behind the proper standing people. The last two albums had pictures that started showing Granddad as a baby and a small child.   Before the end of that album there stood Granddad with his arm around Grandma.   They were both dressed beautifully. Grandma was holding a small bouquet.   Is this their wedding picture?   They, and the cabin, were in the rest of the pictures as what I knew to be his family faded away from the pictures.   And then dad started to appear.

I don't know how long I sat there. I pulled out the small albums and flipped through every page. There were seven of them. The next double door of cabinets had more books stacked neatly, but nothing written inside of them.   Maybe his 'to be read' stash. The last double door set had a stack of ash trays, a neatly folded pile of shirts.   And on the bottom a large wooden box. I lifted it out.   It was heavy.   Carved beautifully with a bird on diagonal opposite ends of the lid. I opened the lid and the aroma of Granddad wafted up to my face. Oh my God. Granddad's pipes and tobacco.   I closed my eyes and let the smell envelope me.   What a sweet, nostalgic, aroma.

I put the lid back on. I didn't want to lose this treasured aroma. Ukko stepped out of the chair and came over. He sniffed the top of the box, my face, and went back to the chair.

This didn't make any sense. This is a lovely little room. Why didn't I know it was a such a wonderful little place down here. I know I hated 'the cellar' as a child. Maybe once the new island was built it was something I just ignored, and everyone else ignored for me.

I went upstairs and got a bucket of warm water with Murphy's Oil Soap in it. Downstairs. Downstairs? What an odd thing to think. I went down and wiped off the cabinets. Everything that wasn't rough hewn I wiped down. Including the floor. It wasn't dirty. Or barely even dusty.

The one lamp seemed to light up the room very nicely. The discovery, or re-discovery, of this room feels almost magical.

I told Ukko to come up. He was very hesitant to leave his new found favorite spot but I finally got him to come up. When he saw me closing the island he barked incessantly at me. I closed the island and opened it again. I loved the design. In the open position the frame worked as a safety gate when working in the kitchen, you couldn't step backwards and fall into the stairwell ,and the island was still useable for the kitchen and the same frame kept you safe from the living area side. The only open side was the end you used to step into the stairwell. In the open position it was more in front of the stove and counter than the sink and counter.

When I closed the island back to its original place Ukko started barking. He was so insistent I had to put him outside. He was not happy. He sat at the front door glaring at me through the glass storm door. He needed to understand I wasn't going to leave it open. I went and let Ukko in, he went right to the end where the steps would be, looked at me with a bit of attitude. I opened the island and he went downstairs. I yelled after him "it's not going to stay open all the time Ukko".

Life at the cabin during my visits here involved outdoor activities with Granddad. Not inside stuff. We slept inside and sometimes ate inside. Hiking and fishing, bonfires and outdoor cooking on the fire were the normal past times when I was here. Sometimes I was here once a year, sometimes several times a year.

After he died I only came here if my parents were here and seldom did I spend the night. The husband had no interest in anything not affiliated with a city. After my parents passed I would come for a rare day here and there. Mostly to just check on it. It dawned on me when I came here after their deaths I was still usually alone. The husband never came with me. I don't think he'd ever been here or would even know how to find it. When I did come here it was either alone or on maybe two occasions with a friend for a weekend getaway.

I went downstairs to find Ukko in the chair. His big body easily accommodated by the size of the chair. "Ukko, what if I want to sit there?" He started to get up. "Stay Ukko".

If the ice sticks around what other treasures might I find around here?

Work kept me busy every day. Keeping the wood stove burning, the wood stocked in the house and lean-to's, and keeping Ukko happy, kept me busy for most minutes of the day. In the evenings I had begun to go downstairs to read. Ukko always sat on the floor when I went down. I didn't ask him to, he just did. I finished "All Creatures Great and Small", opened the front cover and wrote under Granddad's hand writing, my name, the year, and "So did I!"

I randomly pulled out another book. "The Old Man and the Sea" by Ernest Hemingway. "Enjoyed" was written in Granddad's neat script. He read it in 1955. I enjoyed sitting here, reading, like Granddad did. The room felt like a den.   Maybe it was the nostalgia of knowing he sat here, smoking his pipe.   Reading his books. No intrusions from the world. It was another week and three more books before texts were starting to say the roads were passable but snow was coming. The electric had been restored a few days earlier. Today was the third day of sunshine albeit not very long days. I was still doing pretty good with supplies but I took advantage and Ukko and I headed to the village. We stopped at Hammer's on the way. He assured me he had everything he needed. He offered to let Ukko stay while I ran to town.   I offered to Ukko but he had no intention of missing a drive.

We made our rounds.   Picked up fresh vegetables for me.   A fresh doggie cup from the cafe for Ukko. And generally enjoyed being some place not coated in ice. It was a bit of a shock to drive off of the mountain and find the village nearly dry while we were still dripping out of the ice. I stopped at the post office to pick up all of my undelivered mail. There was a good bit. I noticed a couple of hand written envelopes but threw them in the bag I had brought so I could go through everything later.

Driving back up the mountain was like driving to another world. The ice was definitely melting. The temperatures weren't great but the sun was now shining every day. The roads had two tire tracks so if you came across someone both vehicles slowed down and checked to see who had the better ability and room to pull over. Everyone was pretty practiced and patient who lived on these roads.

We got home safely and Ukko bounced around the un-ice-rinked yard while I took everything in and put it away. I grabbed the towel that hung by the front door and dried Ukko and his paws off when he came in. He was as much a clean freak as me and didn't mind getting the dirt and wet off before he came in. I had discovered his need for cleanliness when one day I came out of the bathroom and he stood there with his dog bed dragged over to the washer. I had no idea what he was doing so I picked it up and put it back. He dragged it back and barked at the washing machine. "You want it washed Ukko?" He barked. Hesitantly I unzipped it and took the cover off, putting it in the washer. He barked what could have been a 'thank you' and walked away.

I sat on the couch with the bag full of mail. Ninety percent of it was junk and was just passed from the bag to a pile to be tossed in the wood burner. Then there were bills. A wedding invitation. And a letter. No return address. I opened it. It was from him. Funny I didn't even recognize the handwriting. He asked how I was. Told me he thought he should let me know he was getting married. Thankfully the wedding invitation was not to his wedding, but how ironic. I thought 'good for you'. And added the letter to the burn pile. I had no emotions. I was surprised he even thought he had to let me know. The letter was burnt without a care or any further curiosity.

Ukko barked by the front door wanting to go out again. I let him out and went out to sit on the top step.

Ukko was sniffing everything that was freed from the receding ice. What a beautiful animal. When he stopped moving and stood still I was glad I had my phone in my hands. I took his picture. He was full coated. Tall. Strong. The world behind him was shimmering which made him look all the more solid.

I sat there long enough that I was near froze but Ukko was content out here. The day was turning dark. Clouds were coming. I swear I was turning into an old mountain woman when I said out loud "Ukko, I smell snow coming".

We woke up the next morning to several inches of snow and more coming down. Ukko flew off the steps into the snow. His happy season. Our favorite hiking season.

By the end of the work day everyone at the office had been sent home. A 'snow day' was issued the next day. Though not expected to work, I did.

One of the neighbors sent out a text saying they would be having a bonfire, snow or not, this weekend. Anyone able to come was welcome. Anyone who wanted to come but didn't have a way let the group know and someone would get you.

I ended up picking Hammer up because his ATV wouldn't start. We arrived to a snow made wonderland. Half igloo type structures had been built around the fire pit (large enough to park a truck in). The half igloos had chairs or benches. One of the igloo domes was full of food and drinks, everyone deposited their contribution on the tables. We were all amazed. We sat in groups around the fire wrapped in blankets, some had furs.

I met Mika that night. Ukko stayed by my side. He didn't seem to mind Mika but he wasn't ready to fully trust him either. That came with time though. Hammer and Ukko both stayed close. Protective. Mika moved here recently because of a work transfer. He didn't live on the mountain but 'almost' as everyone teased him. Any interest I'd had in men up to now had been short lived and lived out. This felt different from the get go.

Mika was interesting. Intriguing. He traveled a lot for work and he could weave a tale about those travels that captivated me. Ukko loved Mika's attention. When Mika started coming to the cabin Ukko was welcoming but not very excited about his spending the night. Never, when Mika stayed, did I look over the edge of the bed to see Ukko looking back.

Never, when Mika stayed, did I tell him about the cellar that I had started calling 'the den'. Nor did Ukko bark at the island to go down like he did when it was just the two of us and the island was closed. I think he understood that was just for us. I started to understand why Granddad, and maybe dad? Kept it secret. I had no desire to tell anyone about it.

Mika and I saw each other for two years, when he was home, he traveled a lot for work. After two years he was offered another transfer and promotion, to Japan. He asked me to go with him. I was grateful to be asked but I had no desire to leave the mountain. Or Ukko. We said our goodbyes with fondness. I knew from the start it wasn't going to be a forever thing with Mika. But it was a lovely thing.

I quickly discovered during that two years that as large as the cabin was, it suddenly felt too small whenever Mika stayed more than a day or two. Which was rare. I couldn't at this time see myself sharing this space with anyone. I think Ukko agreed.

I enjoyed Mika's company but when he moved it didn't feel wrong. I was very happy for him. He loved the adventure of new places and things yet seen. At one time I would have jumped at that kind of opportunity as well. But being here felt full of opportunities I would never have experienced had I not moved here and become part of this place. We separated and wished each other nothing but happiness and success. Our successes were just defined differently. And we both knew that.

VIII.

Our community was rocked a year or so after Mika left when Hammer passed away. He was well into his 80's. He had talked with me and others about his fear of having to live anywhere other than on his beloved mountain. We feared the same for him. We had started to take turns visiting him daily. Between us all, we didn't have to go more more than once every ten days or so. But most of us paid him a visit on more than our 'scheduled' day. It was almost a relief when he was found, sitting in his chair facing his best mountain view. At first appearing to be asleep, it was discovered he had passed away while sitting with the company of his beloved mountain. His last dog lying by the side of his chair, forlorn, but peacefully keeping watch until someone got there. Though we would all miss his mountain wisdom, humor and knowledge it was a relief that he wouldn't have to go live somewhere else. His and our biggest fears is that he would end up in a nursing facility where his views consisted of walls, and fresh air would be the air in the closed off courtyard.

We all gathered with his last surviving dog when his ashes were spread on the mountain he lived, and died, on. It was a moving scene when we realized all of our dogs had sat with Hammer's dog throughout the event. Someone had taken a picture of the dogs as they faced the mountain with Hammer's urn between them and the mountain. They sent it to all of us. If I ever needed to know compassion I could always look at this picture.

That night I sat outside with Ukko.
The air was warm with a soft breeze.
You could smell tree and earth.
Ukko puttered around the yard but
not with any zest or intention. He
eventually came up the steps and
dropped next to me, his head on his
paws. I ran my hand over his head.
I don't know what Ukko was
thinking but I'm pretty sure he was
sad and knew Hammer was gone.

I stared at the sky so dark and yet so
lit up with stars. Stars were
shooting across the sky. That black
but kind of purple-blue sky. Streaks
of light blazing in their tininess that
made me wonder how large they
actually were that I could see them.
If even for a few seconds. Maybe
that's all we are here. Shooting
stars. Bright for a second, then
gone.

What a hole his leaving left in our worlds.

VIIII.

What are the freaking odds.

I sat in my truck with Ukko. We had just finished his vet appointment, ate at the cafe, and then picked up his order of food at the post office. We were getting ready to leave the village when I see a man get out of a car. An almost familiar man. He walked to the passenger side of his car and opened the door. Helping a woman out. She kissed him lightly, he closed the door and opened the back passenger door, leaned in, and helped a young child out.

Married and has a child. And here. Surely a coincidence. Watching him I wasn't even curious. But I also didn't want to be seen. I didn't want to feign excitement or interest. I waited for the little family to walk into the cafe I had eaten in and left less than twenty minutes ago. I waited until they were inside before I drove on and passed the cafe as I left the village.

I wasn't worried. I knew without a doubt he wasn't here for me. It was just a coincidence. And if he had been looking for me no one I knew would tell him how to find me. He's a stranger. To them and me.

Oddly though. As we passed the cafe Ukko stood on the seat, looking out the back window of the truck into the cafe, looked back at me, and back to the cafe again.

This dog is super intuitive.

"He's just a stranger Ukko. I didn't know him once before and I don't know him now." Ukko settled into his regular position, seated on his haunches, riding shotgun. Watching out for things I need to pay attention to.

X.

The den was without a doubt Ukko's, and my, favorite place in the house. I eventually put another chair down there so I could have a place to sit without making Ukko move. I was going to take the new chair but Ukko claimed it as his own. I wondered if it was because it sat lower to the floor. I did like being able to sit where Granddad had sat. I had added a picture of Ukko, and one of me and Ukko to the small framed pictures Granddad already had there.

I had finished all of Granddad's books and started adding my own books bought from second hand stores.

Ukko was slowing down. He seemed to be as powerful as ever but not as spritely. It took me by surprise when I realized he was over eight years old. That we had lived here together for over seven years. Many of our neighbors had become family. Hammer's old house was finally sold by his attorney. A young family had moved in with three dogs. Hammer would have loved that.

I went on a vacation with my oldest friends. We went to a beach on the east coast. The young family in Hammer's old house were very agreeable to keeping Ukko for a week. I took Ukko there almost every day for two weeks to get him used to them. Fortunately he loved the children and the dogs. The parents were bonus back scratchers. I explained on the day I took him and left him there that I would be back. His reaction when I went to the truck without him was not unexpected. He followed me. I knelt on the ground in front of him and took his head in my hands. "I'll be back Ukko. I'll only be gone a week. And you like it here. You won't like where I'm going. It's too hot. You stay here." I stood up. He leaned into me. Suddenly he stood on his back legs and put his paws on my shoulders. I think he was taller than me. He licked my cheek. Dropped, turned and went to where the kids were standing waiting for him. He didn't try to get in the truck when I got in and left.

It was a nice week. Hot. Too much alcohol. Too much sun. Plenty of laughs. Not enough of anything that would have kept me away from the mountain and Ukko any longer. My friends knew. I would contemplate doing it again. But not for awhile.

When I drove back into the driveway, of what I would always

think of as Hammer's house, to get Ukko in the early afternoon after flying home he was standing outside with the kids. He went up to each of them and licked them. The parents brought his bowls out and his leftover bag of food. We talked for a bit while Ukko stood patiently waiting.

We got in the truck waving and barking at the waving and barking family.

When we turned onto the road and headed home Ukko dropped on the seat and sighed dramatically. I do believe he was exhausted. He got home, ate, and slept until the next morning.

He was still always eager to go visit but I think another week there would have aged him considerably.

XI.

Ukko and I shared a horrific experience. My hope is that Ukko didn't understand it.

We had gone for an ATV ride and ended up parking at the head of our favorite trail. Instead, we crossed what passed for a parking lot and went in a new direction. I don't know if it was my idea or if I had just followed Ukko.

I had my backpack with water and food for both of us. It was unseasonably cool but warm enough to only need a t-shirt for the climb. This trail led us out to the edge and ran along the rim for quite some time. I'm not necessarily scared of heights but I am scared of standing on the edge of a cliff with no room to spare for mistakes. When it got too narrow I cut up into the woods and walked parallel to the trail until the trail cut back into where I was walking.

We stayed on the trail until it came back out to a very large rocky area. The stone of the mountain was like a layered terrace. I could walk out ten or fifteen feet, step down to another rocky layer, go over some uneven but pretty smooth rock to another layer. Stepping down was far enough I could sit on the layer I had been standing on and put my feet down. "Let's stop here Ukko." I got his water out for him and took a long drink of my own. The view was beautiful. Before me lay a patio made by nature and past that was a vista of mountains and clouds and sun and trees. No matter how many times I saw these views they impressed me into a reverie of gratitude and free thought.

When putting my bottle back in the backpack I saw something bright orange to the far side of the rocky area my feet rested upon. It was a backpack. I watched it for some time. There was no one else up there or around. Ukko sat next to my hip, pushing into me, as he was apt to do. He loved being close. After twenty minutes or so I stood to go over to the backpack. Ukko stood to go with me. I told him to sit and stay. "Not safe Ukko". Going to the backpack meant going closer to the edge. He sat. Unhappily.

I walked over to the backpack. It appeared to be laid out carefully, with a heavy stone on it. That was odd. I got an unsettling feeling. Sticking out from under the stone was a sealed ziplock bag that had what looked like a note in it. I pulled the plastic bag out from under the stone. It said "Goodbye". I looked at the note and back to Ukko who raised his head up higher then stood up. "Stay Ukko". He sensed my fear.

I walked back to Ukko with the note in my hand. He sniffed it. I sat back down. My hand was shaking. Ukko put his paw on my hand. "I hope this is a joke Ukko." The view suddenly felt more foreboding than beautiful. I think I knew it wasn't a joke. There was nothing funny about it. I didn't open the ziplock bag. I just held it. "Stay Ukko." I went back to the backpack and carefully lifted the stone off of the backpack. Without lifting the backpack I unzipped it. The back of my neck went cold. Inside were more ziplock bags. Without taking them out I could see there was a larger gallon size bag with envelopes, letters, in it. On top of that were smaller bags. One had car keys. One had a cell phone. One had a wallet. I closed the backpack and put the stone back on it. For some reason it registered how expensive a backpack it was.

I went back to Ukko. My hand still shaking I called 911 on my cell phone. I gave the trail name and how far up we had hiked. Then waited.

Two rangers arrived and I explained everything in detail. The rangers, having less fear of the edge than I, went to the edge and looked over. They didn't indicate if they saw anything. A rescue/rappelling team were called in. The rangers had gone through everything. I stayed back on my ledge, then moved even further back.

Ukko had remained calm and close to me. Though friendly and loving the attention of the others as they showed up, he was subdued.

I wanted to leave. Once the ranger and then his supervisor got all of my information, and had me repeat my story a few times, they told me I could go, or stay, it was up to me. We left.

Ukko and I hiked back to the ATV. As I drove away I heard the helicopter.

I couldn't get it out of my head. The face of the young man's driver's license the ranger showed me, asking me if I knew him. I did not. Ukko and I sat on the porch late into the night. We could hear the helicopter. Finally, at dusk, we could no longer hear it. I knew they were going to find him.   Inside that bag were too many goodbyes. Too many hearts were waiting to be broken by those letters. It was too neat and too thorough. Someone did not want to be here.

It was a very long time before I went hiking again.

XII.

The den was our evening routine. Not having been a lover of reading for most of my life, while dedicating myself to reading Granddad's books, I was hooked. One day while reading I was struggling with focus and kept reading the same passage over and over again. Finally I read it out loud. I finished and continued to read.

Ukko barked. I glanced at him but continued to read. He barked again. "What?" I lay my hand with the book in it on my lap.

He stepped out of his chair and came over to me. He nudged the book. "What?" He nudged it again. "Ukko I don't know what you want." I picked it up to read. He nudged it. "I'm reading Ukko!"

He stood there while I glanced at the book trying to read but I was half looking at him. I read the same passage again. And again. I read it out loud again, frustrated. When I started to read out loud Ukko went back to his chair. Put his head down and closed his eyes. I stopped reading out loud. He barked. I read out loud, he closed his eyes.

So started the nightly reading to Ukko. Most times I found it charming. On occasion I found it a chore. One of the best things about reading is the silence of the outside world while you take in another world. And I didn't like the sound of my voice. But I did get a kick out of Ukko wanting to be read to. No one else had an Ukko. I finally figured out if I read to him for about ten minutes, it was enough. He would then either be asleep or allow me to read quietly for myself. He seemed to like Hemingway, Patrick Taylor

and books I had begun searching out
that talked about hikes through the
Appalachian Trail and other
through-hike adventures. I'm sure it
probably had more to do with my
voice when I read different genres.
But I like to think he actually had an
opinion.

When Ukko and I went back to hike
for the first time after find the
orange backpack it was well into fall.
Another season. We went to our
favorite spot. Parking in the same
place we parked when we found the
orange backpack. I had been
tempted to do something symbolic
like take flowers up to where we
found the orange backpack. For one
reason or another I decided against
it. When we got out of the ATV I
stood for a few seconds still debating
on hiking up there. Ukko however
had other ideas. He stood next to me

and pushed me, away from where I was looking. I looked down at him. He wasn't being aggressive. But protective I thought. He pushed again. When Ukko pushed you couldn't stand still. I moved in the direction he pushed. Opposite of the last hike we took.

We took our favorite trail and I believe we both felt a sense of renewal. I don't think Ukko understood what happened when I found that backpack. But I do believe he understood the last hike we took was not pleasant. There was sadness and fear associated with it. I don't think he wanted to revisit that.

So we didn't. We went to the place that still stunned us both.

We stood. In awe. In peace. "Just look at that Ukko."

XIII.

Through a small chain of events involving needing my propane tank filled, a new propane delivery guy and having my ATV stuck in the mud of spring I met Conal. He was delivering the propane, I had gotten the ATV stuck in mud coming through the woods into the yard. Conal was filling my tank. He came over and helped me get unstuck. I offered him lunch. He was hesitant. Ukko nudged him. He accepted. We had peanut butter and jelly sandwiches with peanut butter and bread I had made myself and jelly from one of the neighbors. We finished off a cake I had baked. When he left I was standing on the porch as he pulled the big truck with the oblong tank on the back, away. What a wonderful unexpected joy our lunch was. He stopped at the curve, and backed up. I went to the truck and he opened the door and jumped down.

"I have your number because of your order and account. But I wanted to ask...can I use it to call you?"

This big, auburn haired, grizzly man was blushing through his beard. My "of course" was accompanied by a blushing smile. He tipped his baseball cap, as I've seen done in the movies only, and jumped back in his truck. He stuck his head out of the window. "Then I will."

And he did.

It felt different with Conal around then it did with Mika. It's almost as if Mika was an interlude to what life was at that time. And Conal was what life was supposed to be.

Our first date started at the cafe but ended with us on the other side of the mountain at a lake I had not been to. We would visit that lake time and again as our special spot. Ukko and Conal's dog Lady Bug (a sheltie) were both with us. The dogs were hesitant around one another initially. It didn't take them long to look like they had known one another forever. If Conal ever showed up without Lady Bug, Ukko would run to the door, see that Lady Bug wasn't with him, then ignore Conal for as long as Conal would be there.

Conal had a camper and we started going camping on long weekends. Our second summer together we took a three week road trip. Three full weeks of being with someone 24/7. Looking back at that trip I realized it was what cemented us.

On our return from that trip we were together more than we were apart.

Conal had his own place. A small property with a small home and a large barn. He was very much the outdoor man he appeared to be. He looked like a lumberjack. He always smelled fresh as the outdoors. He loved to chop wood and between the two of us we chopped a lot of wood. His garden was something to be jealous of but I didn't have to be. He taught me as I began helping him.

I felt as much at home at his place as I think he felt at mine. Home felt homier when he was there. I remember the first time I read to Ukko when Conal was there. He had sat on the floor leaning up against Ukko's chair. Lady Bug sat next to Conal. I felt weird for the first minute or two. But it quickly

became a part of their routine.   It
was now ours. All of ours.

XIV.

Ukko is getting older.

He's almost 11 years old.   That sounds so insanely young.

He walks slower.   He doesn't romp. We've resorted to more ATV and truck drives.   Hikes have been reduced to 'walks'.   Though I call them 'hikes' to make sure he feels like he isn't missing out on anything.

We read every night. I have come to look forward to it every evening.   I read   out loud longer, even after he has fallen asleep. I take the steps in front of him to help him when we descend into the basement.   I walk behind him to make sure he can get back up the steps.   It won't be long before he can't come down here any more. That will be a sad day.

He still loves to be close. Sitting on my feet even as I stand in the kitchen cooking or doing dishes. Which makes for some interesting acrobatic moves on my part to lean and reach without disturbing him.

Every morning he greets me as I peek over the edge of the bed.

He makes me laugh, still.

He just makes everything better.

One night we were sitting around a fire. Conal and Lady Bug, me and Ukko. I had to go inside for a minute. When I came out Conal was kneeling by Ukko, holding Ukko's head in his hands. I don't think I've ever seen such a moment like this between man and dog. I stood back. Conal was promising Ukko he would take care of me and make sure I was always loved. Ukko put his face to Conal's face. I knew that Ukko trusted Conal. But it didn't occur to me that Ukko needed reassurance. And it didn't occur to me that Ukko needed to hear that for any reason.

But he did.

Conal and Lady Bug have all but moved in. We still spend a lot of time at his place taking care of the farm. He thought about renting out his house and calling my cabin home but we just haven't gotten there yet. It's coming though. We've both been through a divorce and neither of us wants to go through it again. We both agreed to be patient, and take it slow and steady.

It's nice to see Ukko have a buddy. They are great companions. It seems like Lady Bug knows Ukko is aged, and struggling. She doesn't romp or pounce around him. If they are outside together she walks slowly with him. If she is outside without Ukko she runs and jumps and skitters around.

When Ukko started to struggle more with steps we built a ramp on the porch so he could still get in and out with less struggle. Unfortunately we couldn't do the same for the den. When Ukko could no longer go up and down the steps I stopped going down there to read or relax. I stay upstairs with Ukko. I read in the living room or outside if it's nice. A couple of times Conal carried Ukko down to the den for me but that didn't seem to be easy on Ukko. So we stopped doing that.

Right now life is as perfect as it can be. Conal and I love the mountains, our dogs and each other.   Ukko and Lady Bug are the best of friends.

We will enjoy this sense and feeling of perfection for as long as we are granted.

XV.

I lost Ukko today. Though my heart is hollow at the moment I cannot wish him to still be here. That wouldn't be fair to him. He lived longer than expected but not as long as I hoped. I believe in life after here. And I believe he is a part of it. I hope he is bouncing in the snow. Greeting all of his friends that went before him. I know he has returned to his full and powerful stature. His heart never diminished over the years. It kept up with his soul. And nourished mine.

I know come tomorrow morning I will wake, expecting to see him as I peek over the bed, as I have for the last 12 years.

What a graceful existence he lived.

What a better human I am because of him.

I hiked up to our favorite place one last time with him. Conal and Lady Bug joined me. Ukko's ashes in my backpack. I brought a book with me thinking I would read to him one last time. As I sat there with Ukko's ashes I couldn't bring myself to read it out loud to him. It didn't seem fitting. Instead, I thought of a Will Rogers' quote. I opened Ukko's urn and walked with him to the very edge. I couldn't look down. I could only look up. With tears I paraphrased Mr. Rogers' quote. "Ukko, if you aren't in heaven, when I go, I want to go where you have gone." I let the ashes flow out and over the edge. The wind taking them out further. Away.

You're safe now Ukko. And thank you.

Where you can find all of my books:

lulu . com